Secret Fear

Mohamed Sheriff

Published in 2019 by
Sierra Leonean Writers Series
Warima / Freetown / Accra
120 Kissy Road, Freetown
Kofi Annan Avenue, N-Legon, Accra
Publisher: Prof Osman Sankoh (Mallam O)
Email: publisher@sl-writers-series.org
Website: www.sl-writers-series.org

Pampana Communications
104 Campbell Street,
Freetown
Email: msaydia@gmail.com

ISBN –978 -99910 – 54-74-2

First published in 1997 by Macmillan Education

Copyright© Mohamed Sheriff 1997, 2019
Design and illustration© Pampana Communications

Chapter 1

Musa Kabba and his two young sisters, Khadija and Rugi, sat in the quiet hall of the Mama Gintay Maternity Hospital. None of them spoke. They were all praying silently for the life of their stepmother. Fati was in trouble, and so was her baby. Only an operation would save her and the child.

A door opened and a nurse passed through.

"Is she... ? Is the baby... ?" Musa could not say the words. The nurse shook her head. Things were not going well. Fati was fighting for her life, but how could she tell these poor children?

"There's no news yet. The doctor's doing the operation now. I'm sorry."

Khadija and Rugi started to cry. It was as if the nurse had said Fati would die. Musa had to hold back his own tears as he watched his sisters. He wished that their father was here. He would have known what to do.

But Foday Kabba, their father, was far away, lying in a hospital bed himself. He had been badly hurt in a road accident just the week before, hurrying to get home to his family. Now Musa had to pull himself together and be responsible. He was the eldest child, the only son—unless the new baby was a boy.

Just a few weeks ago Musa had been a happy student in his first year at university. Now he was head of the family and the family was in terrible trouble. What if Fati died? What could he say to his father? And how could they live without Fati, their dear stepmother?

Thoughts of life without their "little mother" flashed across Musa's mind as he waited anxiously. Khadija and Rugi were also remembering the sad days they had once known.

"Do you remember before...before Fati came?" said Khadija softly. "When Mother left?"

Musa remembered only too well. Their mother had gone away to America and soon afterwards they heard she had married another man. Their father had no money at that time, and he was often silent or angry.

"You were only ten years old," Musa told her. "You didn't understand what was happening."

"I knew that Father's business was bad and I missed Mother so much. I wanted to die when she packed her things and left. Why did she leave us, Musa?"

Musa tried to answer. "She hated being poor, I think. But Father did his best. He missed Mother too, I'm sure. It was a bad time for all of us."

"Do you remember all those cousins and all those maids?" Rugi interrupted. She was only eight years old when Olive, their mother, left them, and she had never forgotten those unhappy times. One of their father's cousins had come to stay, but none of the children liked her. After two months another relative came. She only lasted a month and then there were different maids all the time.

"Father was miserable, and so were we," Musa said quietly. He had not thought about the bad days for a long time now. "But then Fati came into our lives."

"She saved us," Rugi said. "That's what Father told me."

They could all remember that special evening. They had been studying at the big table when their father walked in with Fati.

Khadija smiled through her tears as she remembered. "She was the most beautiful lady I'd ever seen," she said. "She had the sweetest smile and the whitest teeth. Her eyes seemed to be smiling, too. She took our hands and said our names as if she'd known us all our lives."

"She kissed me on both cheeks," said Rugi.

"And she hugged me," added Khadija. "I loved her at once. It was as if the sun came out suddenly after days of dark, rainy weather. I knew then that everything would be all right."

It had all happened five years ago but Musa, Khadija and Rugi remembered it as if it had been yesterday.

"Remember how she lifted me on her lap?" said Rugi. "Then she asked me questions about my school and my friends and about home."

"And she asked me for a glass of cold water," Musa smiled.

"Yes, and as you ran for the water, Father laughed for the first time in ages," added Khadija.

It was as if they had known Fati all their lives. From that day onwards, she had become a part of their family. She came to live with them permanently a few months later when she married Foday, their father.

And now they might lose her, this lovely, loving person who had changed their lives. She was still a young woman, and she had borne Foday two babies, but they had both died at birth. Would this third child live? And if the child lived, would the mother die? They all knew that she was not very strong.

"Let's pray for Fati and her baby. That's all we can do," Musa told his sisters.

Musa was still buried in thoughts about his stepmother and praying anxiously for her and her child when the door of the waiting hall opened again. Musa turned and stared into the grim face of the doctor.

Doctor Bayoh was a close friend of his father. As he walked towards Musa, the boy's heart started beating wildly. What if Fati had lost her baby? What if the child died? It would be the third time—surely it would kill her? Worse still, what if mother and child had both died?

Musa pushed back the wave of panic that was coming over him.

He must be brave. He stared closely at Doctor Bayoh's worried face. He could not guess what his father's friend was thinking and he did not dare ask. He stood up and his legs felt weak. He gripped the doctor's arm.

"Are you all right?" Doctor Bayoh asked. Then he saw what was happening to the boy—he still did not know the news. "It's

OK, Musa. They're fine, both mother and child are well. He's a healthy baby boy. Fati's still in the operating theatre, but they'll both be fine."

Musa hugged his sisters who were weeping for joy. "Thank God! And thank you, too, Doctor Bayoh. Thank you so much."

A nurse appeared from a room opposite. "A telephone call for you, doctor."

"Thanks, I'll be there in a minute. Musa, you're the eldest son. Since your father's not here you can come with me and have a look at the child. You can only stay for a minute though." He turned to Khadija and Rugi. "Come back tomorrow, girls, and you can all see Fati and your new brother," he told them.

Both Musa and the doctor returned to the hall moments later.

Musa was grinning happily, but the doctor had a worried frown on his face.

"He's such a big child! The nurse says he weighs eight pounds nine ounces," Musa told his sisters. Then he noticed the frown on the doctor's face. "What's wrong, Doctor Bayoh? What's happened? Is there a problem? Is Fati...?"

"Your stepmother's fine. But the phone call—it was very strange. Someone rang to ask whether the child had been born yet. Then she—I think it was a woman—asked whether Fati and the child were both well."

Musa waited. The phone call did not seem strange to him. All their friends would want to know the news.

"So... ?" he asked politely.

"When I asked who was speaking, the woman put the phone down immediately," the doctor continued slowly. "I thought that was odd. But what was really strange was the voice. It was as if the woman was speaking through a handkerchief. It was as if she didn't want me to know who she was."

Musa went cold as he listened to the doctor's words. Could somebody want to harm Fati and her child? And why? Fati was the best, the kindest person in the world.

"Do you have any idea who would have done that?" the doctor asked, interrupting Musa's thoughts.

"None at all, doctor," he replied. He could only guess himself.

He was worried. Surely nothing could happen to Fati and his new brother?

"It's probably nothing," said the doctor. "But even so, I wish your father was here."

Chapter 2

The woman, was angry, bitterly angry. Her hands gripped the steering wheel as the car rolled silently down the drive. She had left her home as soon as she heard the news, unable to wait a moment longer.

She pulled the car out onto the narrow dirt track and coasted down towards the main road. Then the car gathered speed. She had always feared driving at night on this road, with its dangerous bends and steep drop into the valley below. Tonight she forgot all that.

She had to see Pa Kante, the medicine man at Lumpa village. And she had to see him at once, even if she had to wake him in the middle of the night. He had lied to her. He had promised that the child would not be born alive. And for that promise she had paid him half a million leones.

Yet Fati and her baby were both alive. That was what the doctor had told her over the phone. And the woman did not know what to do next.

"The old liar," she said to herself angrily. "One thing's certain, I've got to see him now, tonight."

As she drove through the centre of town the woman thought again of Fati, Fati who had everything—beauty, a happy marriage to a rich husband, stepchildren who loved her dearly.

She raced past the Clock Tower and onto Kissy Road, tears running down her face. At first she had just been jealous of Fati. Then another feeling took over—hate. As long as Fati had no child· of her own she could control it, but now the child had been born. Fati had a son.

She brushed away the tears. Along Waterloo Road there was hardly any traffic, and the only light came from her own car and the few cars driving the opposite way, into the town. The houses were few and far between, and away from the main road. Away on her left and behind her, lights shone faintly from the ships waiting in the calm waters of the sea.

At Waterloo she had to stop briefly at a checkpoint. A policeman with a woollen cap pulled over his ears and a torch in his hand inspected the car. Then he waved her on.

After that the road was rough with potholes, so she was forced to drive slowly. She also had time to think!

Pa Kante's compound lay in a dark, lonely area, along a narrow track with only a few houses nearby. Now the woman was deep in the country. Still she drove on, her car brushing the bushes on either side where the road narrowed to a footpath. Nothing could stop her. Twice she lost her way and had to go back again. The last hundred metres, however, were level and straight.

There were three buildings in Pa Kante's compound. The house was in the middle. It was low, and painted bright green, with a veranda and a corrugated iron roof.

Her lights lit up the front of the house as the car drove into the compound. She sounded the horn of the car until the door swung open. Pa Kante, in a dirty white gown and holding a lamp in his hand, stepped onto the veranda.

He was used to late-night visitors and was not surprised to see the car. He waved to the woman to get out but she did not move. Lumpa was famous for poisonous snakes—and snakes terrified her.

Pa Kante was now certain who was in the car. Although the woman did not know it, he had already found out exactly who she was. He always found out as much as he could about his visitors.

He also knew why she was back. The child had been born, and born alive.

As Pa Kante walked towards her car, the woman leaned over the front seat and unlocked the door. He slid in beside her. He sensed that there would be trouble. He knew it without question.

Suddenly the woman felt sick. She always felt like this when she was near the medicine man. She pressed down the button that opened the window on her side.

"Open that window," she ordered stiffly. She felt better as the cool air filled the car.

"Good morning, madam. A surprise visit," Kante said, trying to smile.

"Fati has a son," she hissed in return.

Pa Kante tried to stay calm as he felt the force of her anger. "I know," he answered quietly.

"What do you mean?"

"I know that the child has been born."

"I paid you half a million leones and all you can tell me is that you know?" The woman's voice rose in anger and carried far into the silent night.

"Please, calm down. You don't want our neighbours to hear you," he said gently.

"How can I be calm, when... when you... you promised," she said and burst out into tears.

Kante waited. When she was quiet again, he spoke. "Madam, you never really trusted me, did you?"

"No I didn't. But I don't blame you, I blame myself," she said bitterly. "Just be prepared to give my money back, every cent of it.

The medicine man nodded. "I'm sure that that's not what you came here for," he pointed out coolly.

"So why am I here?"

"If you only wanted your money you'd have waited until tomorrow. You wanted something else. You came to find out whether there's anything I can still do about the baby. And the answer is: Yes, there is."

The woman knew that Pa Kante was right. It was not just the money. She still hoped that he would come up with something, a new plan, a different idea. She still wanted the baby to die.

Now full of hate as she was for Fati, jealous as she was of her, this was a terrible thought. Wishing for the child to be born dead was one thing. Killing a living child was another.

Kante read her mind and smiled. "You're thinking that would be murder, aren't you?"

She nodded.

"No. It won't. When this child dies it won't be murder. You see, he isn't properly alive, even though he seems healthy. Half of his life has left his body already. The other half will leave soon. He will never live to have his naming ceremony. Everything will be over very soon. Trust me, I know what I'm doing."

"Are you sure?" she asked. She wanted the child to die, but she wanted no part in murder.

"Yes, I'm quite sure," he smiled at her. "The child will die, I promise you."

"Well... all right, then. As long as it's not murder."

Pa Kante shook his head. "It's not. But one more thing. You may see my wife Orya at the hospital or at the Kabba house. You know her, don't you? If you can make things easier for her... "

"No!" The woman shouted out loud. "I don't like this—I don't want to be connected with you."

He could not look her in the eye. He knew she meant trouble.

She was different from his other visitors. They needed and respected him. This woman felt none of this.

"If that's how you feel... " His voice rang false in her ears. "My wife doesn't really need you. I only told you about her to put your mind at rest. These are things you don't understand, magic things. Just trust me. Everything will work out."

The woman looked hard at him. "If you fail?" she asked.

"If I fail, I return your money. I haven't touched it," he lied. Neither of them spoke. All around them were the sounds of the night—the frogs, the insects, the whisper of the wind in the trees.

The woman turned and stared at the medicine man. He was small and dark, with deep-set eyes and a wide mouth. Kola nut and tobacco had stained his broken teeth.

How could people trust such a man? And why did she hate him so much?

Suddenly, looking at him, she knew the answer. She hated him in the same way that she hated herself. She was no better than this terrible man. Both of them were wicked, evil people.

"Get out," she ordered, and as he opened the door she whispered, "Don't try to make a fool of me. I'm a woman, but I can be hard when I choose to be. With all your secrets and your medicine and your magic, I can still destroy you."

Kante looked into her eyes. He knew that these were not empty words. He said nothing as he slid out of the car and shut the door.

The child must die, he thought.

Chapter 3

The strange feeling began when Fati's visitors arrived. They were all there—Hawa, Fati's own sister, Isatu and Bintu, her husband's sisters, and so many friends and neighbours that she could not count them. Even Olive, her husband's first wife, had come.

The women chatted and laughed together. The baby lay sleeping in his cot. And the mother lay without moving as fear gripped her heart.

Fati could not listen to the talk around her. She could only think of her child.

"Oh God, don't let anything happen to him," she prayed silently.

Somehow she knew that he was in terrible danger. Something evil· was coming.

After all the visitors left, the feeling became even stronger. She tried to sleep, but evil pictures filled her dreams. She saw Foday, her husband, in a burning aeroplane. She saw witches waiting to eat her child. She could not save either of them.

In the cot at the foot of her bed a little brown snake wriggled beneath the blanket. The baby, his arms folded across his chest, slept on.

The snake was trying to escape from the blanket on which the baby lay. The baby turned in his sleep and moved his right arm. The snake wriggled angrily.

Soon the snake escaped from the folds of the blanket. Now it waited just a few inches away from the baby, its head turned towards one bare arm. Still the baby slept on. The mother sensed the evil, but finally, exhausted, she fell into a deep sleep.

When Nurse Theresa came into Fati's room a few minutes later she was carrying a tray of medicines. She pushed the door open quietly and moved towards the bed. She did not want to wake the sleeping mother yet.

As she crossed the room, her eyes fell on the little brown snake with its head so close to the baby. She opened her mouth to scream but no sound came out. She only just managed to put the tray down on a table beside the bed.

Then Musa entered the room behind her. He frowned as he saw her. "What's wrong?" he asked.

Nurse Theresa could not speak. She pointed a shaking finger at the snake lying still in the cot.

Musa stared and his own body became weak. The baby moved. The snake wriggled again.

Musa recovered a little from his shock. He pushed past the nurse and stood beside the cot. He hardly dared to breathe as he watched the baby and the deadly snake, for he was sure that the snake could kill.

Only one thought was in his mind. Fati's only child must not die. Doctor Bayoh had said she could never have another.

The baby moved again and Musa's body grew stiff. He must act now, immediately. A moment's delay and the child would be dead. He shot his arms forward like a strong spring and gathered up the child as the snake struck the air. He pressed the child into the shaking arms of Nurse Theresa, grabbed the cot with the angry snake still inside and rushed out of the room.

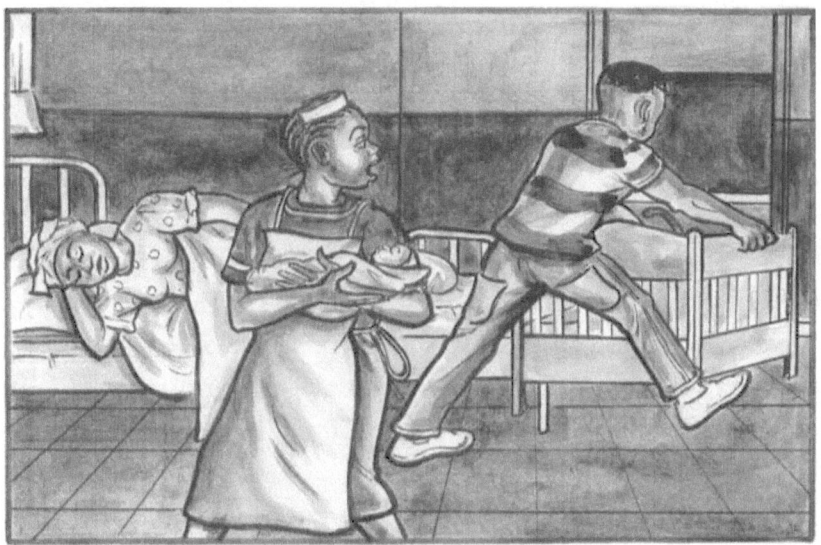

In the hall outside Fati's room Musa pushed past Doctor Bayoh as he headed for the stairs. He took the steps two at a time, holding the cot as far away from his body as he could, until he crashed through the main doors of the hospital. Out on the lawn he threw the cot down. As the snake wriggled towards the bushes he grabbed a stick from a visitor and beat the snake on the head again and again and again.

Musa felt weak and faint as he slowly climbed the stairs back to Fati's room. In the hall outside he found Doctor Bayoh and Nurse Theresa. His father's friend was questioning the nurse, but he stopped as Musa came up.

"Is it dead? Did you kill it? Nurse Theresa told me what happened."

"It's dead. It won't harm anybody now."

"Was it poisonous?" Nurse Theresa asked Musa.

"Very poisonous. I knew what it was. It's called Ekparamoleh."

"Ekparamoleh!" the doctor repeated. "That's one of the very worst." He turned back to Nurse Theresa.

"You entered the room and found the snake lying in the cot beside the child?"

Nurse Theresa nodded, "Yes, doctor, and Musa came in right behind me."

"Thank God," the doctor said, his face grim. "One thing's certain—the snake didn't get there by itself. Somebody put it there."

"No!" Musa cried. He had been so anxious to save the child that he had not thought of how the snake got into the cot. If somebody had placed the snake there, it could mean only one thing.

"Doctor are you saying that somebody tried to murder the child?" he asked at last.

"I can't think of another explanation," Doctor Bayoh replied. He turned to Nurse Theresa. "Did Mrs Kabba have several visitors today?"

"Yes, doctor," Nurse Theresa answered. "1t was not long after they left that I entered the room. We can thank God that I did, and no harm was done. The danger's over now."

"But it's not," the doctor said with a worried frown on his face. "That's what worries me."

"You mean... you mean they'll try again, doctor?" Musa asked anxiously.

"Why not? Somebody who smuggles a snake into the hospital and leaves it in the cot must want the child to die. There's a murderer about, and I'm sure he'll try again."

"He... or she," Musa said softly. He thought for a moment and his voice became fierce. "We've got to stop it."

"I'm not worried about the hospital," said Doctor Bayoh. "It won't be difficult to protect the child here. I'm worried about what happens when your stepmother leaves here. Unless the man's caught and stopped, he'll keep on trying."

"I'll find him and stop him," Musa said. "I won't let anybody harm Fati, or her child."

The doctor wished he were as certain as Musa. He was deeply shaken. He knew how badly Foday and Fati wanted this baby. He had to do all he could to save him. He turned to Musa.

"Do you have any idea who could have done it?" he asked. "Think carefully."

Musa thought for a while and then shook his head. He had several people in mind but he was not going to tell a stranger, even Doctor Bayoh .

"Don't talk to anybody about this," the doctor said at last. "I'll speak to the head of the hospital security guards, and ask him to guard Fati day and night. He'll find out what he can, but let's keep this a secret for now. OK?"

Musa and Nurse Theresa nodded.

"Musa, you'll have to do a lot of work outside this hospital because you know your family well. I'm sure the answer to this problem lies there. I don't think we'll find out much more here, and Fati and the child will be safe as long as they're in the hospital. But we've got to find out who put the snake in the cot. Fati will go home soon."

"Nurse Theresa, would you recognise Fati's visitors if you saw them?" asked Musa. "I'd like to know who was here."

The nurse shook her head. "Perhaps one or two, but not all. I do know that they were all women. Your stepmother will know them."

"I don't think we should ask her," Musa said. "She'll be worried."

Doctor Bayoh agreed. "You're right, Musa. It will be too much for her, especially at night. She's had a big operation and she's not strong."

"I know this is foolish, but I've thought of something too," said Nurse Theresa.

"What is it?"

"Suppose this thing was done by some sort of magic? I know you people don't believe in such things, but it's possible."

A long silence followed. Nurse Theresa might be right. The doctor had read and heard about medicine men and their magic. Could he ignore Theresa's idea?

"God is more powerful than the medicine man and his powers. We'll pray to him. He'll protect Fati," Musa said.

Doctor Bayoh again wished he felt as certain as Musa.

Chapter 4

At home, Thursday, 8th April, 8.00 pm

When Musa told his sisters about the snake, Khadija and Rugi both burst into tears.

"You mean... you mean somebody tried to murder the baby?" Rugi whispered.

"Yes, I do. It's a terrible thought, but it's true. Somebody tried to kill the child." Musa thought for a moment. Then he said slowly, "But I think he really wanted to hurt Fati."

It was difficult to calm Khadija and Rugi down after that.

"Now be quiet and listen to what I have to say," Musa said gently.

Both girls looked up at him.

"We've got to save both their lives," he went on. "If anything happens to the child, Fati will die. But with the help of God, we'll stop the murderer. He'll try again, no doubt about that, so we have to be ready."

He took a deep breath before he went on. "The hospital is safe, Doctor Bayoh's taken care of that. There are guards in the hall to watch Fati's room round the clock. They'll search the bags, baskets or parcels of any visitor to her room. She'll be safe from snakes and everything else there. The problems will·

start when Fati and the baby come home—unless we can stop the murderer,"

"So what should we do?" Rugi asked. "I'll do anything."

"First of all, can you think of anybody who would want to hurt Fati? Or the child?"

Khadija and Rugi thought hard.

"There's Auntie Isatu," Khadija said at last. Isatu was their father Foday's sister.

"Auntie Isatu? You don't mean it."

"Rugi, we've got to think of everybody if we're going to save Fati," Khadija told her sister. "I know it seems horrible to suspect our own family, but Musa's right. The person who tried to kill the baby's got to be somebody close to us. And Auntie Isatu never wanted Father to marry Fati. She thought that Father was too old for her. She's always complaining that he never has time for anybody else. She's jealous because Fati's younger than she is and so beautiful."

"If we're thinking of Auntie Isatu we've got to think about Auntie Bintu too," Rugi added. Bintu was their father's other sister. "She didn't want Father to marry Fati either. And now she says that Father loves Fati too much. She hates it whenever Father gives Fati a present."

Musa knew at once that Khadija and Rugi were right. His aunts didn't like Fati. They blamed her whenever anything went wrong.

"I can think of somebody else who hates Fati," he said slowly. "Auntie Hawa, her own sister. Everybody loves Fati and Auntie Hawa can't bear it. Remember when Fati's parents were so ill, just before they died? They came and stayed here and Father paid for the nurses to look after them. Auntie Hawa knew that their parents loved Fati best. She was horrible about it."

Khadija and Rugi were nearly in tears again. Musa tried to stay calm, even though he felt ill with worry. He was head of the family for the moment. He had to do the right thing.

"Don't cry," he told his sisters. "Fati and the child need us. We can't help them if we're crying ourselves. Now you're not to go anywhere for the next few days. If any of those three aunties, or anyone else, visits the house, watch them closely until they leave. And stay with Fati when she comes home, in her room."

"You mean somebody might try to hide another snake in her room?"

It's possible, Khadija. It seems a stupid and dangerous thing to do since nobody can control a snake. It could bite anyone. But if somebody hates Fati so much, it could happen," Musa explained.

"Then none of us is safe," Khadija said.

Rugi was thinking hard, and there was a frown on her face. "Musa, you said they can't control the snake. What if they do so by... by magic?" she began.

"Clever girl, Rugi," Musa said, "I've thought of that. I find it hard to believe in magic, But just in case, we'll pray, right? We're good Muslims. We know that God is the greatest."

"That's true," Rugi said, feeling better at the thought.

"Musa," Khadija said, "this is terrible. We can't watch Fati and the baby all the time. It's impossible. Somebody could slip the snake into the house in the middle of the night when we're all asleep."

"I've already asked for two extra guards. They'll watch the compound, and everybody who comes in and out. But I want to find out who this person is before Fati comes home."

"And how are you going to do that?" Rugi asked.

Musa was not sure.

"Leave that with me," Musa said. "You two can help by keeping your eyes and ears open and watching all the aunties."

There was silence for a minute, then Khadija asked slowly, "What if it's someone else? What if it's not any of those three?"

"It has to be one of them. It has to be someone close, and I can't think of anyone else."

"I... I can."

Musa and Rugi stared at Khadija.

"What do you mean?" Musa asked.

"Who?" added Rugi.

"It could... it could be—Mother?"

"No!" cried Rugi at once. "Mother was glad that Father married Fati. She sent a card and a letter. She asked Fati to look after us as if we were her own children. The letter pleased everyone, especially Fati. I remember it all."

"I know that," Khadija told her sister. "But look what happened afterwards. Exactly six months later the largest diamond in the history of the country was found in one of Father's mines. He became one of the richest men in the country." Khadija took a deep breath.

Musa and Rugi were listening now. "And that's when Mother came back," she added. They all knew that their mother's other marriage in America had failed and she wanted their father to marry her a second time.

. Musa nodded. "But Father was happy with Fati."

"But the aunties weren't—they wanted Mother back," Khadija went on. "They said Father was a Muslim and Muslims can have more than one wife. They said that Mother had made a mistake, but she was sorry for it. They said Father should forgive her."

"That was just because they hate Fati," Rugi interrupted.

"I know that, Rugi. But remember how they said that Mother had been a good wife to Father for a long time? They said that now he was a rich man she should share in his success, even though she had made a mistake."

"And in the end they agreed," Rugi said. "Father gave Mother that beautiful house at Hill Station and enough money to start a business. She was happy with that, wasn't she? After all, she gets along well with Fati. I'm sure she's glad that Fati takes such good care of us."

"Rugi, I know this is hard," said Musa gently, "but Khadija could be right. Mother seems to like Fati, but she could just be acting. Fati's happy with Father and she's rich and beautiful and everybody loves her. Mother's alone now, and I don't think she's very happy. Perhaps Mother does want to hurt Fati."

"No, no, no!" Rugi almost shouted. "It couldn't be Mother!"

"We just don't know," Khadija said. "What we've got to do is find out quickly. This thought of a snake around the corner will keep me awake at night."

That reminded Musa about something.

"Don't tell Fati anything about the snake," he warned. "She'll have bad dreams even during the day."

"Then we must do something, and do it fast," Khadija said.

"We will," Musa replied.

Chapter 5

Musa drove along the winding road towards Lumley in his father's car. If he was going to discover the mystery of the snake he had to speak to each of his aunties. He had no idea how he would do this without arguing with them, but he was going to try as hard as he could. He had three aunties and each one had her own problems.

It was difficult. What would he say? He could not just say, "Auntie, somebody tried to murder our new brother with a snake and I suspect you."

It would never do. He could picture his Auntie Isatu. She would insult him or even throw things at him as she chased him out of her house.

Or Auntie Bintu. She would put her hands to her head, and sit in the middle of the sitting room, crying and blaming her brother for everything.

And as for Auntie Hawa or his own mother—he could not bear to think of what they would say.

He had to be careful.

All too soon Musa found himself in Lumley and turned into the dusty road towards his Auntie Isatu's compound. It was hidden among trees, off the road. As he turned into the narrow drive, he could see her new car parked in front of her beautiful concrete house.

He thought about the cars. His father had bought new cars for Isatu and Bintu and also for Musa's mother, Olive. Even this did not please his sisters. Instead they became even more jealous of Fati, because she had a bigger car. They said that their brother had insulted them by buying them smaller cars. Whatever Foday did was wrong.

Only his mother seemed pleased about her car. She had thanked Musa's father for it very happily. Why could his aunties not behave like that?

As Musa waited impatiently downstairs he looked around Auntie Isatu's house. His father had bought beautiful furniture for it, and Auntie Isatu had chosen exactly what she wanted. Still she was not satisfied. Still she complained that Foday did not do enough for her and the rest of the family.

"Auntie Isatu should be happy," Musa said to himself. "She owns a good business, a beautiful house in Lumley. She's got a husband who loves her too."

But then Musa remembered. Auntie Isatu had no children, and her husband wanted a child badly. Was his Auntie worried about this? She loved her husband dearly, and wanted to stay with him. Perhaps the man was planning to marry somebody else, a woman who would give him children.

Could this be the reason why Auntie Isatu did not want Fati to have a child?

He heard the sound of Auntie Isatu's footsteps as she came down the stairs.

"Good morning," he said politely.

"What can I do for you, Musa Kabba?" she asked taking a seat.

She smiled at him.

She seems cheerful, Musa thought and sat down by her. He looked closely at Auntie Isatu. She was usually a large woman with a pretty face, but she seemed to be losing weight. Why was she thinner these days? She was certainly very attractive. She loved expensive clothes and jewellery, and was wearing gold earrings, rings, bracelets and chains with her beautiful wrapper.

Musa knew he had to speak. It was best to come straight out with it.

"Auntie, yesterday somebody tried to murder the new baby by putting a poisonous snake in his bed," he said suddenly. "A very poisonous snake—it's called Ekparamoleh."

"What!" Auntie Isatu exclaimed. "A snake in the baby's bed? How did that happen? How did it get there?" She really seemed worried—but could Musa believe her?

Perhaps you placed it there, he thought to himself. Or perhaps Auntie Bintu did. Or perhaps it was that crazy sister of Fati, or perhaps even his own mother. Only God knew.

"This is what I'm trying to find out."

"Then why have you come here?" Auntie Isatu asked suspiciously. "Why are you talking to me about this snake?"

Here we go, Musa thought. He tried to remain calm himself and said, "I wanted to tell you, since Father's not here: Can we put our heads together and try to solve the mystery?"

"Have you told your mother?"

"No, but I'm going to, and Auntie Bintu too."

"I see. Do you have any idea who could have done it?"

Musa looked at his aunt, then he shook his head and said, "I can't think of anybody."

"Are you sure about that? Do you suspect us—me and my sister?" she asked angrily.

"Why would I have such a horrible thought?" he lied.

"Because your father has been telling you and your Fati how much we hate her. I'm sure that we were the first people Fati thought of. She's sent you to find out, hasn't she?"

"No Auntie, Fati doesn't even know about the. snake. Doctor Bayoh and I decided not to tell her, because it will only frighten her," Musa

explained carefully. He waited and then began again.

"It doesn't mean I suspect you," he continued. Things seemed to be getting out of hand. He could see his auntie getting angrier and angrier. She would explode at any moment. "I only want to talk to you. Perhaps you noticed something. You were in the hospital yesterday, weren't you?"

"So what!" Auntie Isatu jumped to her feet. "You see what I was saying? You're questioning me like a murderer. I don't blame ·you. It's your father who has been putting words into your ears. I pray that he soon recovers and comes back home. Then I can tell him exactly what I think of him. Now get out. I'm calling your mother right now."

Musa got to his feet.

"Auntie, I was only asking you to help. I've got to solve this mystery. Don't you want to save the child? After all, he's your nephew."

"I don't care! He's Fati's child, and there's no love between us. Fati's asked for whatever she gets. I don't care what happens to that child. Fati sees herself as the richest and most beautiful woman on earth. She feels too good to touch the ground with her feet. She's too proud for her own good. This time she's made a real enemy—me!"

Now who's proud? Musa said to himself and then said out loud, "Listen to me, Auntie Isatu. Fati's the kindest, gentlest and friendliest person I know. If there's only one angel on earth, I know she's the one. I don't know why you hate her so much. You're simply jealous."

"How dare you talk to me like that?" his Auntie shouted, her voice rising and dying in her throat in anger. "How dare you! I carried you on my back, when you were a baby."

Two servants came running into the room at the sound of her voice.

"Go back!" she ordered. "And keep out of here. This is private business."

They disappeared at once. Auntie Isatu had a sharp tongue even when there were no problems to upset her. All her servants were terrified of her. Musa did not feel very brave either at that moment.

"Musa Kabba, leave my house! When you have proof that I tried to murder the child, you can come with the police to arrest me. For now get out!" She rushed at him, slapping him all over his face.

Musa used his hand to protect his face as he backed out of the house. He ran to the safety of his car and headed back to Lumley Road. His Auntie Isatu really was something!

Auntie Isatu stood on her veranda, breathing heavily. She stared after Musa long after he disappeared from sight.

Chapter 6

Musa was not quite sure where to go next when he left Auntie Isatu. Should he go to his mother's house at Hill Station? Or should he visit his Auntie Bintu, who lived nearer? He did not really want to go to either of them.

Then he remembered. It was the middle of the morning. Auntie Bintu would probably be at her shop in the centre of town by now. He would go there first.

He felt that he had handled his Auntie Isatu badly. He knew her fierce nature. He knew that she was unhappy. He had just made everything worse. But what else could he have done?

He was certainly no nearer to finding the murderer.

He drove slowly back into town, past the cotton tree and towards the shopping centre. After he had spoken to Auntie Bintu he would go to Fati's sister, Hawa. He would talk to his mother later.

As he drove along the hot, dusty streets, Musa was thinking again about his father's two sisters. Both of them had a lot to be happy about, yet in their different ways they were unhappy.

They both had successful businesses, beautiful houses, cars and jewels. However there were certain things missing in their lives which made them very unhappy.

Auntie Isatu had a loving husband, but no children. She wanted a baby of her own so badly.

Auntie Bintu had three children, but a good-for-nothing husband. He was amusing and handsome but he was lazy. He spent half of the day in his wife's shop, eating or drinking coffee. He spent the other half in night clubs and beach bars. He never did a day's work if he could help it. Auntie Bintu could not trust him in any way.

Musa felt sorry for both of his aunties. Even so, why did they have to be so jealous of Fati? It was as if his poor stepmother .was responsible for everything that was wrong with their lives.

Or perhaps they felt that Fati should not be happy because they were not happy. Was that it? He drove on to Auntie Bintu's shop with these worrying thoughts in his head.

Musa had no sooner entered the shop than his Auntie Bintu started to complain.

"Your Auntie Isatu called about a quarter of an hour ago. She's very angry with you," she said as Musa walked through to the back of her shop.

She's acting, Musa thought. She's never as calm as this. She must be the one.

"She told me about the snake in the child's cot. She said you believe we hate Fati and we're jealous of her. She said you suspect that we tried to murder the child," Auntie Bintu went on. Her voice was still low and mild. "Musa, how could you think such a terrible thing of your own aunties?"

"I never said I suspected you. I only wanted to find out from you who was at the hospital. I had to ask somebody. I need to discuss this with you."

"Well?" His auntie waited. She was working herself up for something. Musa had to go on.

"Who was visiting Fati yesterday? If we know, perhaps we can find the person who put the snake in the cot. If we don't, he or she will try again." Musa stared his auntie straight in the eyes. She
looked away, then back at him.

"I was there. Your Auntie Isatu was there. Hawa, Fati's sister was there. You mother was there. Some other ladies, perhaps friends of Fati, were also there. I don't know their names. We all left at about the same time."

It was Musa' s turn to wait.

"If the snake was discovered in the cot a few minutes after we left, then one of us must have placed it there," Auntie Bintu went on at last. "Since your father has made it known to everybody that we hate his wife, I don't blame you, Musa. I can see why you suspect us of doing this terrible thing."

At this she burst into sobs and buried her face in her hands. Tears flowed down her face, and her whole body shook.

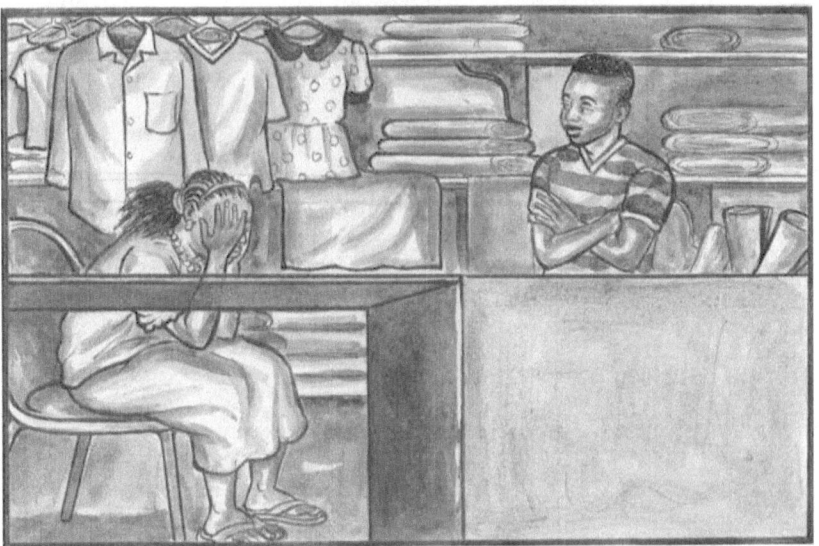

Musa watched her silently. He was not moved in any way by her crying. He was used to this sort

of thing. His auntie could act brilliantly.

She could cry whenever she wanted to. He was only annoyed because he was still getting nowhere.

Auntie Bintu lifted her tearful face to look at him. She opened her mouth to speak.

Before a word came out Musa spoke.

"I never suspected you, Auntie. There's no need for you to cry and sob, You're not helping at all by behaving like this. The baby's life is in danger.

We need to find and stop whoever is trying to kill him. Crying won't solve the problem at all. If that's all the help you can give me, I'm leaving."

Musa got to his feet.

"Sit down." Auntie Bintu's voice had changed. Suddenly it was hard and unfriendly.

Musa obeyed.

Listen carefully," she continued in the same hard voice. "I'd be a liar if I said there's any love between Fati and us. There isn't. But this isn't our fault. It's because she doesn't like us. She can't stand her husband's family. She's spoilt everything between your father and the rest of us. She wants no one around him. She wants to keep him to herself."

"What about us?" Musa asked. "What about me and Khadija and Rugi? She wants us, and don't tell me anything different. I won't believe you."

· "Keep quiet and listen to me," Auntie Bintu snapped. "You don't know anything, You're only a child. Your stepmother knows how much your father loves you and your sisters. She can't do anything about that. She has to accept you."

"No! That's not true. You don't understand, Auntie Bintu."
His auntie did not hear a word he said.

"What's worse," she continued, as if he had not spoken, "she talks about us behind our backs. She says all sorts of horrible things."

"Like what?"

. She stared at him coldly for a while.

"I can see now why my sister was so angry with you, Musa. You never allow people to say anything against Fati. She may be an angel to you, but not to us. She's always going about saying things that just aren't true. She tells people that she doesn't mind us because we're just unhappy old women. She says my husband doesn't care for me. She says Isatu is so stone-hearted because she's never had children. She tells lies all the time."

Musa could not believe this.

"How do you know all this?" he asked.

"Fati's own sister told us. Your Auntie Hawa."

"Then she's lying!" Musa screamed at her. "You want to believe such things about Fati because you don't like her. Everybody knows that Hawa hates her sister."

He had gone too far.

"Look here!" Auntie Bintu pointed a finger at him. "If you scream at me again, the slaps you received from your Auntie Isatu will feel like kisses. If you're not blind and if you're not so stupid, you'll ask yourself why everyone should hate Fati. It's true, Musa. Everybody hates her. Doesn't that tell you that something's wrong with her? Doesn't that tell you that her ways are bad?"

"No!" he said. "It tells me nothing!"

"Get out of here if you won't believe me, you fool!" Auntie Bintu screamed at him.

Musa stood up and left without another word. He felt weak and his legs were shaking.

What could he say? He really had handled things badly. He was nowhere near solving the mystery of the snake. And both his aunties were angry with him.

Even so, he did not trust either of them. Either could be the one who had tried to kill the child. But which? Or they could even be working together. It was too terrible to think of.

Musa wished again that his father was well again and back with the family. He would know how to handle his sisters. He would protect Fati and her child. But the way things were, Musa alone was responsible.

Auntie Bintu watched until Musa stepped out of the shop and disappeared into the crowd. Then she picked up the telephone and began to make a call.

Chapter 7

Musa parked his car in the big compound in Kissy. There were four tall apartment buildings in the compound, two at the front and another two at the back. Once this had been a good address and the owners of the apartments had been proud to live here. Now the buildings were old and dirty. Nobody had painted or repaired them for many years.

Musa walked to one of the apartment buildings at the back where Hawa lived on the fifth floor. He climbed the stairs to the top and pressed the bell and waited.

Soon he heard footsteps. Then keys turned in the lock and the door swung open. Hawa stood there frowning at him.

. Musa studied his auntie. She was tall, and she wore a loose-fitting yellow T-shirt. Skin-tight green trousers covered her shapely legs. She had long hair and a face which had once been very beautiful. Years of wild living and night life had robbed that face of its softness. Now it was cold and hard, with lines which made Auntie Hawa look older than her thirty-five years.

If Auntie Hawa smiled, that face could still be beautiful. At the moment, frowning, it was not.

"Well?"

When Auntie Hawa's eyes met Musa's they were cold and unfriendly. This was not new. It did not surprise Musa. Auntie Hawa hated her sister so much that she also disliked anybody close to Fati. And today there seemed to be more hate in her eyes than ever before.

She's the one, Musa thought to himself. This woman could put a poisonous snake in the baby's cot. She could even stab him with a knife. Look at those eyes. There's no pity there, no softness.

"Good morning, Auntie Hawa," Musa began. Even before she replied he knew this meeting was going to end up like the others. Auntie Hawa was his last hope, and he was suddenly filled with fear.

Why did he always fail? Why did everything always end like this?

He had to solve the mystery of the snake. He forced himself to continue, but before he could speak Auntie Hawa interrupted.

"Don't call me Auntie! I'm not your aunt," she shouted. "And I know why you came here. I had a phone call about twenty minutes ago to tell me."

Auntie Isatu's been busy, thought Musa. Or perhaps it was Auntie Bintu. He stepped back. He had always been surprised that two people who looked so alike were so different. Hawa and Fati were the same height and the same shape. Even their faces were very much alike, although one was ten years older than the other. It was very easy to mistake one sister for the other when they turned their backs. Even Auntie Hawa's voice, when she was not complaining, was very much like Fati's voice.

"I just wanted to ask you a few questions about Fati..."
"Don't!" shouted Auntie Hawa.

"But Auntie Hawa." Musa would not give up.

"Right," Auntie Hawa broke in. "You've asked for it. I'll tell you all about Fati. I always hated her, from the day she was born. She was always perfect and I was nothing. She was the sweet little daughter and I was the naughty girl. She was praised and all I ever got were complaints. Everybody loved and admired her and avoided me."

"But Auntie Hawa..." Musa tried to interrupt, but nothing could stop Hawa now.

"I was slow at school and Fati was clever. Even my own father said that. I dropped out and Fati went on to university."

Musa knew this already. Auntie Hawa had stopped school at the age of sixteen and joined the Bongo Dance Band. She had not even been a singer or dancer, but just one of the girlfriends of the leader of the band. Since then she had made her own decisions and lived her own life.

"Fati got married to a rich husband," Auntie Hawa went on, "and I never married anybody. Why should my people blame me, for that? But they do. People have always blamed me, and my sister has always been perfect. And that only makes me hate Fati more."

Now she looked as if she was about to kill poor Musa.

She's the one, no doubt about it, he thought. He must arrange for the guards to watch her round the clock.

The thought did not make him feel better.

"Are you listening to me?" Auntie Hawa interrupted Musa's thoughts. "I haven't finished yet."

"Yes I'm listening."

"I don't care whether a snake or a poisonous spider or a lion or a monkey was found in the child's cot. Fati's business is Fati' s business and Hawa's business is Hawa's business. I don't care if I never see her again. So don't come to me with your questions and don't tell me what to do. I don't want to hear any more of your rubbish!"

Musa opened his mouth to speak but Auntie Hawa had lots more to say.

"Do you know why I still go near my sister sometimes? Not because I love her, but because I promised my father I would. I promised to keep my hate to myself and not show it to the whole world. I promised I would behave like a sister. That was the only reason why I visited her in hospital and that's why I shall go to the naming ceremony."

Musa was about to speak, when Auntie Hawa took one last deep breath.

"I have nothing else to say to you, Musa Kabba. I have no information for you. If you want anything from me, go to the police. Let. them come and get it from me. Tell Fati to use her beauty, her brains and her money to stop the killer. Goodbye!"

She slammed the door in his face.

Musa remained standing at the door for a while.

He wanted to break down and cry.

The sun was high in the sky as Musa drove back to his own home. The roads were busy with cars and lorries, and the pavements crowded with shoppers. The giant cotton tree in the centre of the city threw its shadow over the people resting below.

Musa saw none of this. He passed the big stores, the traders shouting in the streets, the passengers calling for taxis. It meant nothing to him. He could think of only one thing.

He was the only person in the world who could save Fati and her child. And so far he had failed.

He stopped the car outside his own home. The Kabba compound lay at the foot of a hill, and was surrounded by high walls. He sounded the horn, and a guard came running to open the heavy iron gate.

Beyond the gate, Musa could see the big, white house where he lived with his sisters.

Khadija and Rugi heard the powerful car and hurried out to meet him.

"Did you see the aunties?"

"Did they see anything? What did they say?" The girls' questions

all came out at once.

Musa shook his head.

"They didn't say anything," he replied in a tired voice.

"Oh come on, Musa. They must have told you something," Khadija cried.

She was right. The aunties had told him a lot, not just with words, but with looks and the way they behaved. They had told him how much they all hated Fati.

Khadija and Rugi followed Musa into the cool house. Every room reminded him of Fati. Here was the furniture that she had chosen. Here were the photographs of her parents. Here was the home that she had made for them.

Musa felt exhausted. He called to one of the servants to bring him a cold drink, and sank into one of the deep chairs.

"It was hopeless," he told his sisters. "I didn't get any information that I didn't know already. There's just one important thing to remember. The aunties all hate Fati. They'll stop at nothing to hurt her. Any one of them could have put that snake in the baby's cot. So I'm no nearer to finding out the truth."

He closed his eyes. It had been a long, long morning.

Chapter 8

The house was full of people, as groups of women, friends and relatives of the family, went about their work. They were busily preparing food. The naming ceremony for Fati's child would be carried out tomorrow. Everything had to be ready for the party that would follow.

The woman sat by herself on the top veranda. She watched everything that went on below. Her brain was racing.

She hated the thought of Fati having a child of her own. A husband, her home, stepchildren who loved her, Fati had those already. And now she had a baby, a beautiful little boy. That would complete her happiness.

The woman simply could not bear it. The pain of Fati's happiness was so great that the woman had paid her visit to Kante.

Even so, the woman was not happy. She had agreed to the medicine man's plan, but now it weighed heavily on her. Stopping the child from coming into the world alive was one thing. Ending the life of a child that had cried, had seen sunlight... It had given her miserable days and sleepless nights. Her dreams had been full of fear and terror.

She had felt both glad and disappointed when nothing had happened to the child in the hospital. And now he was home, carried to his cot by his mother.

The woman looked down from her place on the veranda. She could see Orya, Kante's wife, moving about with the crowd. She alone knew why Orya was here—to carry out Kante's orders. Something was going to happen, and soon.

All around her people were happy and excited. They were preparing for the naming ceremony. But somewhere in the house, in a quiet corner, stood a tin box with an angry brown snake in it.

Musa too had a sense that something evil was about to happen. .He had been feeling this way since he had driven his stepmother and her baby home earlier that evening.

As the night wore on, the feeling grew stronger. He knew · disaster would strike soon. Time was running out.

Musa knew that Fati felt the same. Ever since that day when he had found the snake at the hospital, Fati had been waiting for the disaster. He had seen the fear in her eyes, even then. He could feel it again now. His stepmother was living in terror, even though she still knew nothing of the snake, the deadly Ekparamoleh.

His sisters were in Fati's room. They would search the baby's cot and watch over their stepmother. But was that enough? What else could he do to save her?

The crowd was smaller now. Some people were filling their baskets and bags with food and drinks as payments for their work. Others would stay the night and help again in the morning, before the guests arrived. Among those who were staying the night were all three aunties, Isatu, Bintu and Hawa.

The enemy would strike either tonight, when they had all gone to bed, or tomorrow, after the naming ceremony. Either way it would be difficult to stop the disaster.

Up until now Musa had not talked to his own mother about the snake. He was certain his aunties had not told her either. If Olive knew she would have spoken to him.

He got to his feet. He would discuss everything with her.

Perhaps his mother would have some suggestions. She might know what to do. He had to talk to somebody or he would go mad.

As Musa hurried to the veranda where his mother had been sitting by herself all evening he had an idea.

"Why didn't I think of it before!"

He could not stop himself from speaking out loud. He clapped his hand to his mouth. He must not speak his thoughts out loud. In his own house he could trust nobody.

Now Musa's brain was racing. The person who wanted to kill the child must know about snakes. Or, at least, know somebody who was an expert on snakes. Only an expert would know about a snake which was small enough to slip in a child's cot but poisonous enough to kill, a snake like the little brown Ekparamoleh.

Who was the expert? A snake charmer perhaps? Or one of those people who sold snakes as medicines or to bring good luck? Or even a medicine man?

Musa was sure that there were not many snake experts in town.

He was also sure that they would all be well known. But how could he find out who they were? And how could he find out which of the experts were honest men and which were criminals?

Musa forgot all about his mother. He hurried to the car. Not far away, in the little tin box, the snake awoke.

Standing near the house, Orya breathed a sigh of relief. The gate of the compound opened and the car drove through it and turned onto the road.

Musa had gone away, and he was the danger. She had taken care not to cross his path. She was afraid that he might become suspicious. Now that danger had gone. Now she was certain that everything would be easy.

That morning Orya had smuggled the tin box, with the snake inside, into the house in her bag. She had found a perfect hiding place for it, at the back of a dark cupboard. Nobody would find it there.

She had waited all afternoon. She wanted to slip into Fati's room when it was empty, and when nobody would notice her. But Fati was never alone. Her friends and family were with her all the time. Her two stepdaughters never left her side. The child slept peacefully in his cot at the foot of the bed.

Now at least Musa had left the house. Soon everybody would find a place to sleep for the night. She had to act now, before it was too late.

Orya thought fast. She knew that this was her chance. How could she carry out Kante's plan? If she failed he would beat her again and again. She had no choice about what to do. She had to obey his orders.

Soon an idea came to her. There was a can of kerosene near the garage at the back of the house. There was also a large pile of wood in the compound nearby. Orya had noticed it there earlier. And best of all, this part of the compound was dark and secret.

She knew what she had to do next.

Nobody saw her walk to the back of the house. She removed the can of kerosene from its place near the garage, and carried it over to the pile of wood. Next she poured the kerosene over the wood, taking care not to splash her wrapper. Then she took out a match.

She worked silently as she quickly put the lighted match to the wood.

The whole place brightened as the pile of wood turned into one great flame. Orya slipped into the shadows as silently as she had arrived.

"Fire! Fire!" somebody screamed.

She cry was caught up by others. Soon everyone was rushing to the scene. What had happened? How had the fire started? How could they stop it?

Orya ignored the fire. She hurried straight for a dark cupboard in a corner of the house. She collected the tin box, hid it under her wrapper. She dashed up the stairs as both Rugi and Khadija rushed down.

She stood in the hall upstairs, in the shadows near the door to Fati's room. She waited, smiling to herself when Fati went out onto the veranda. The child was wrapped up in a blanket and Fati carried him tenderly in her arms.

Orya left her slippers in the corridor and crept on tip-toe into Fati's room.

Soon her work was finished, and she vanished into the night.

Chapter 9

Fati watched the fire from the top veranda, but she did not stay there for long. The pile of wood burnt out quickly. The night air was heavy with smoke. She pressed her baby close to her in his blanket.

She soon returned to her room. As· soon as she entered she felt the sense of evil again, far stronger than it had been before. And yet the room was empty. Nothing had been disturbed.

Fati held the child tenderly in her arms and started to shake. She could not stop herself. Even though she had Musa, Khadija and Rugi she felt so alone and frightened. If only Foday could be here'

The woman had seen Fati as she watched the fire from the veranda. She saw the child too, sleeping peacefully in his mother's arms. So he was safe. Orya had done nothing. Kante's plan had failed.

The woman was almost glad.

As the fire died down, the woman followed Fati back to her room. She did not know what drove her to do this. It was as if some other power was in control of her body.

She caught up with Fati at the door of the room. Fati was still shaking all over. The woman's heart stopped for a moment at the sight of Fati's pale and frightened face and the tiny baby in her arms.

"What is it? What's wrong?" she asked in a whisper.

"I—I'm so afraid. I feel... I feel something terrible's going to happen to my baby. I know it. He's in danger, terrible danger. If only Foday... "

Tears were now rolling down Fati's face. "Please," she said in a weak voice, "please hold the baby. I know he'll be safe with you."

Fati held out her son to the woman. The woman took the child in her arms and held him against her body. He was warm and soft and his smell was sweet.

The woman knew at that moment that she had lost the fight against Fati. There was no way that she could harm this child. There was no more hate for. his mother in her heart. She could never allow Kante to hurt this baby. Her mind was made up. ·

"Go back to bed," she told Fati. "You're safe with me. I'll stay with you and protect the child. It's all over. Nothing will hurt the child now."

The woman meant every word she said. She was no murderer.

She would find Orya and stop her. Kante could keep his money, every penny of it.

She was sitting next to Fati on the bed, quietly singing a little song to the child, when Khadija and Rugi returned from the fire.

"Here you are at last," she smiled. "Fati's worried about the baby. She thinks something evil will attack him. I've told her there's nothing to fear."

"That's what I've been telling her too," Khadija said. "But she's been upset ever since he was born."

"I wish Father was here. He'd know what to do," said Rugi.

"He would," the woman agreed sadly. She knew Foday, and she knew how true those words were. She turned to Fati.

"Rest now," she said gently. "No harm will come to your baby. He's safe in his own home."

"Will you stay with me?" Fati asked. "I feel better when you're with me. And after all, you're one of the family."

"Please stay," begged Khadija and Rugi.

The woman stood up, the child still in her arms. She laid him down gently in his cot. He continued to sleep soundly.

"I'll stay for as long as you need me," she answered.

Under the folds of a blanket the little brown snake stirred and wriggled.

The woman stayed in the room until Fati fell asleep. Fati's fears had lessened, but the woman herself was far from calm. She wanted to go out and find Orya. She had to stop her. She had to cancel whatever it was that Kante had planned. She would have nothing more to do with the medicine man and his evil ways. ·

The woman got to her feet. Fati and the child were sleeping peacefully, and even Rugi's eyes were closing. She could no longer sit here doing nothing. She must find Orya and stop whatever she was doing.

"I'll be back soon," she told Khadija, and pressed her finger to her lips to silence her.

"I'll explain later," she continued in a whisper. "Stay here with Fati and the child. I'll be back soon," she added and left the room quietly.

The woman knew the house well. It took her almost half an hour to decide that Orya was not there. In this time she searched the living rooms, the bedrooms, cupboards, kitchens, bathrooms, and everywhere else she could think of.

Next she started on the compound. It was a dark night, the sort of night that the woman hated. Clouds were building up before a storm, and the air felt hot and heavy. There were no stars and no moon to light the sky,

The woman was strong and brave, but it took all her courage to go outside. Only the need to find Orya forced her on.

Her mind was full of pictures of snakes, insects, spiders, and all the animals of the night. Her own father had been killed by a poisonous snake, and she had never been able to shake off her fear of them. She forced herself to continue her search.

"Has anybody left the compound?" she asked the guard at the gate. He stared back at her stupidly. He was almost asleep himself. "Has anybody left the compound?" he repeated after her. "Who do you mean? People have been coming and going all day. I don't understand who you mean."

He was right. She had asked a foolish question. She tried to think clearly. What had Orya been wearing? She had to describe her to the guard.

She tried again.

" A woman," she began. "A tall woman, with a very dark skin. She was wearing a blue wrapper with big square patterns. She had a head-tie to match."

The guard shook his head.

"That could be anybody," he said. "I don't remember her."

The woman walked back along the drive to the house. She had to think. She had to decide what to do next. But she felt tired and miserable and she just did not know what to do. She sank down on a metal chair and started to sob.

The little brown snake was wide awake and angry.

From the window of Fati's room Khadija was watching. What was happening? What was wrong? She had to find out. She would go downstairs and into the compound. She would only leave Fati and the child for a minute. Musa would not be angry about that. He would understand. Nothing would happen. After all, Rugi was still with them.

Khadija slipped out of Fati-s room and ran down, the wide stairs.

The woman was still sitting on the metal chair on the veranda.

"What's going on?" Khadija asked. "I saw you speaking to the guards. Why were you searching the compound? What were you looking for?"

The woman could not keep any more secrets. She felt a pain as if a sharp knife had been stuck into her heart.

"I don't know," she sobbed. "No, that's not true. I do know. I was looking for Orya, one of the women who were here earlier. She's... she's going to harm the child. I've got to find her. I've got to stop her. Please, Khadija, help me."

Khadija's eyes opened wide. She could not believe what she was hearing. Suddenly she understood everything.

"You!" she cried. "It was you, wasn't it. It was you who tried to kill the child."

"Yes... No... "The woman could hardly speak. "I wanted the child to die... but now... Oh, Khadija, you must help me. Forgive me. I was so wrong, so wicked, I know that now. What can I do? How can I save the child?"

Khadija' s heart melted. She placed a gentle hand on her back.

"Tell me everything," she said.

Chapter 10

When Musa drove out of the compound in his father's car he had already decided where he was going. There was one man who would know about snake experts. That man was Inspector Fofana, one of his father's friends. He would have some ideas.

Musa drove down the hill and onto the main road. He could see the sea on his left as the road twisted and turned. Not so long ago, this area had been one of quiet villages and small farms. Expensive houses like his own had been built in the last few years, but the road here was still little better than a rough track.

Musa wished that his home was nearer to the centre of the town. He had no time to waste if he was going to save the child.

Luckily for Musa, Inspector Fofana was in his office when at last he reached the police station. The Inspector agreed to see him at once. Musa told him the whole story.

"So you see," he finished, "the snake must have been put there by an expert. Somebody who knows all about snakes. Somebody who could chose the right one, and know where to find it. Somebody like a snake charmer or a medicine man."

"You're right!" Inspector Fofana exclaimed. He banged his fist on the desk. "Some medicine men are good and help people, and others are just the opposite. You're looking for one who's a criminal, and I've got a good idea who he is. I know who would most likely be behind this type of thing. It's Pa Kante at Lumpa village."

Musa had never heard of Pa Kante. "Pa Kante?" he asked. "Who's he?"

"Kante' s a very clever medicine man, but he's also one of the wickedest people I've ever met. He's interested in money and power and nothing else. We've been wanting to catch him out for a long time now. Unfortunately the people who know about his evil

ways won't come forward. They're all afraid of him."

"Let's talk to him," said Musa. "Where does he live?"

"In Lumpa village," Inspector Fofana told him. "Have you got a car? Then let's go. There's no time to lose."

Musa and Inspector Fofana drove past the cotton tree and the large shops, and along Kissy Road. It was now quite dark, but the street markets were as busy as ever. Musa thought that they would never leave the traffic and the city behind.

They picked up speed when they reached Waterloo Road. A wave of the hand and they were past the police checkpoint. Then they were really in the country. The Inspector had been to Pa Kante's compound in Lumpa village many times before, so even though it was dark, he could give Musa directions.

"How are we going to make him talk?" Musa asked. "He'll pretend he doesn't know anything."

"That's always been our problem," the Inspector told him. "But this time things are different. He's part of a plan to murder a child. We've got to be as clever as he is. We can't let him get away with this. We've got to put an end to his evil once and for all."

The lights were on in Pa Kante' s house when at last they arrived at his compound. Musa parked the car in deep shadows behind the house.

When they walked round to the front of the house the door was already open and Kante was standing on the veranda. They did not know, but he was already a worried man. His wife had not yet returned. He did not care very much what happened to Orya. He did not love her and he beat her often. But he did want to know whether she had carried out his orders.

Pa Kante was surprised to see Musa and Inspector Fofana instead of his wife. He was not, however, afraid of them.

"Come in, Inspector," he said. "Welcome to my house again. What can I do for you tonight? Introduce me to your young friend please."

"This is Musa Kabba, the son of Foday Kabba." If Pa Kante was shocked he did not show it.

"We want to talk to you about something very serious," Inspector Fofana went on.

"Yes?" said Pa Kante. "Murder."

"Murder? I don't understand. Why speak to me about murder?

I'm only a poor medicine man. I know nothing about murder. How could I know anything?"

Inspector Fofana took a deep breath.

"Last Thursday somebody carried a snake into the Mama Gintay Hospital. The snake was placed in a baby's cot."

"A snake? In a baby's cot? How terrible," cried Pa Kante. "Was the child hurt? Was it a poisonous snake?"

His voice sounded innocent, but Musa knew that the medicine man could not be trusted.

"No, the child was not hurt, and yes, the snake was poisonous," Inspector Fofana went on. "It was an Ekparamoleh. We have reason to believe that you were responsible."

"Me? Responsible? Last Thursday you say? But

I was here all day. I can prove it. Ask any of my neighbours, they'll tell you. I never left my compound. I'm a poor old man. Why do you say these terrible things?"

"Neighbours can lie, or make mistakes," said Inspector Fofana in a hard voice. "I tell you, Kante, we believe you were responsible."

"Then prove it." Suddenly Pa Kante's voice was hard. "Did somebody see me at the hospital? Did somebody see me carrying a snake? Who gave you this information? You see, Inspector, you can prove nothing against me."

Musa knew that Pa Kante was right. They had no proof.

"I have come here to arrest you," Inspector Fofana was saying.

"You will come with me to the · police station. You will be questioned there."

"You can arrest me and you can take me to the police station, but you cannot keep me there. You say I'm a murderer. Then prove it. You can't."

Musa could not bear it any longer.

"Pa Kante," he broke in, "why did you do it? Did somebody pay you money? I have to know. Who was behind this plan? Who's really responsible?"

Pa Kante laughed in his face.

"I shall tell you nothing. Nothing, do you hear? And you can do nothing to me."

Musa and Inspector Fofana both knew that he was right. They needed proof, real proof.

At that moment there was a noise of a car outside. The noise became louder as the car drew nearer to the house. Suddenly Musa had an idea. He grabbed Inspector Fofana' s arm.

"Quick," he said. "Let's hide. If Pa Kante' s visitor thinks he's alone he may say something. We may get our proof even now."

"You're right," said the Inspector. He pushed Pa Kante into the only armchair in the room.

"Sit there," he told the old man. "And don't warn your visitor that we're here. This is one conversation that I want to hear."

Musa and Inspector Fofana slipped into a back room as the car stopped. They heard voices, and then the noise of a car leaving.

"It must have been a taxi," breathed Musa. "I hope nobody saw my car."

Seconds later they heard footsteps outside, and then the front door opened. Who was it? Would they learn anything? Would they get the proof they so badly wanted?

A bag was put on the table, and then the voice spoke.

"I did it, Kante. I obeyed your orders exactly. I put the snake in the Kabba child's cot."

That was it! That was their proof! They had got what they wanted!

Musa and Inspector Fofana burst into the main room.

"You're both under arrest," shouted the Inspector. This time he pulled Pa Kante up from the armchair. "You're coming to the police station with me. And you won't be coming back here for a very long time."

Musa was staring at the other person in the room, the person who had spoken to _Kante. It was a woman, a tall, dark woman wearing a blue wrapper and head-tie. There were big, square patterns on the wrapper.

He had seen that woman earlier that day, in his own home. "Quick!" he screamed. "I've got to get home. The child's in danger. I've got to save Fati's baby."

There was a strange smile on Pa Kante' s face, a cruel, evil smile. "Wait, Musa Kabba," the medicine man said. He knew that he had lost, but he still had one last trick to play. "Have you forgotten something?

Don't you want to know who's behind all this. Don't you want to know who paid me to do it? Don't you want to know who's really responsible?"

Musa waited. There was a long silence, and then Pa Kante spat out a name.

"Olive. Your own mother, Olive."

Chapter 11

Musa drove back to the house alone. He left Inspector Fofana with Pa Kante and Orya at the police station. The Inspector had tried to telephone the Kabba home, but he couldn't get through.

So there was no way for Musa to tell his family of the danger. He could not warn them about the snake. He would just have to get home as quickly as he could and pray that he was in time.

"Drive as fast as you can," Inspector Fofana told him. "Don't stop for anything. Good luck, Musa."

Musa's hands were shaking on the steering wheel as he drove through the streets. Olive, a murderer? Olive, his own mother? How could she be behind such a wicked, wicked plan? How could she even think of killing Fati's little baby?

How would Khadija and Rugi accept such horrible news? And what would Foday, his father, say when he knew of his mother's plan?

Yet the more Musa thought of it, the clearer everything became.

His mother must have been mad. It was the only way to explain what had happened.

Musa knew that his. mother's life was unhappy. Her second marriage had failed, and she had no husband to love her. She saw her three children happy with their stepmother, her first husband happy with his new wife. Poor Olive had understood too late what she had lost.

That was it! When his father refused to marry her for a second time it must have driven her mad.

But at the moment there were other bigger things to think about—like saving Fati's baby.

The tyres screamed as Musa headed across the town.

Back at the house Khadija had her arms around her mother, as Olive sobbed her heart out. Khadija held her tightly. She had forgiven her already. Her mother had made a terrible, terrible mistake, but that was what it was. A mistake, and nothing else.

And she was sorry for it, anybody who saw her now would know

that. A good Muslim would forgive her.

"Tell me everything," she said again, when her mother's sobs lessened.

"I was so jealous of Fati. I couldn't bear the thought of her having a child so I went to a medicine man."

"A medicine man?"

"Yes. His name's Pa Kante. He lives in Lumpa village. I wanted him to kill the child before he was born. He said he would, but his magic didn't work."

"And then?"

"Then when the child was born alive I went back to him again.

He told me that the child was not really alive. He promised that he would die before the naming ceremony. And the naming ceremony's tomorrow. And Orya's here, I saw her earlier. But now I can't find her and I can't stop the magic."

Olive was sobbing again. Khadija did not really understand what she was saying. She took her mother by the shoulders and shook her. She had to know the truth before she could save the child.

"Who's Orya?" she asked. "What magic?"

"Orya's—Orya's Pa Kante's wife. She was here this afternoon. I saw her myself, but now I can't find her. I've got to stop her. She was going to bring the magic to... to kill the child."

Khadija' s brain was working fast.

"What magic, Mother? Another snake? Did Orya put the snake in the baby's cot when he was in the hospital? You've got to tell me.

Her mother stared at her.

"I don't know anything about a snake. But if there was a snake in the child's cot, then yes. Orya must have put it there, but I didn't know that. Do you think she... could she? Oh no, surely not!"

Khadija acted before her mother could burst into tears again. She grabbed her by the arm.

"If you can't find Orya she may have put another snake in the baby's cot already. Quickly- we must move now!"

Khadija and her mother rushed back to Fati' s room. The light threw soft shadows over Fati and her child, sleeping peacefully. Rugi opened tired eyes as her mother and sister entered the room.

It was Khadija who first saw it, crawling on the blanket on top of the child. She pointed with shaking fingers. Rugi let out a weak cry, her eyes widening with fear.

Their mother put her fingers to her lips. Nobody must make a sound. Nothing must disturb the snake.

Olive moved past Khadija, who was looking about her for something to beat the snake, and took silent steps towards the baby's cot.

The girls held their breath as they watched the woman, their own mother, move slowly but surely towards the cot and the snake. They knew that a snake had killed Olive's father. They knew how much she feared snakes. They knew how brave she was to do this.

Olive was shaking so much that by the time she got to the cot they thought she would fall on the snake and the child.

She bent over the cot, and with one hand quickly took one side of the blanket, and folded it backwards. Then she brought the edges of the blanket together with her other hand. The snake wriggled angrily, but it was trapped. The child slept on.

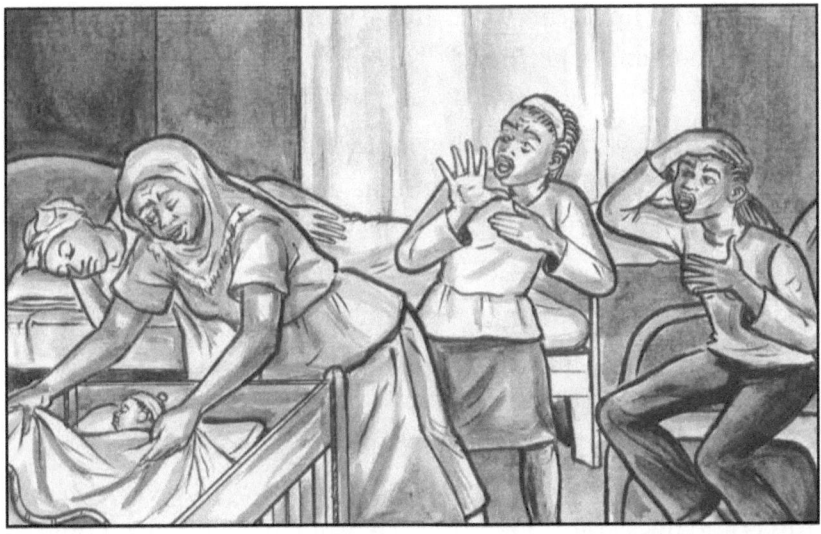

Holding the folded blanket with both hands, Olive rushed towards the open door and along the corridor. Down the stairs she ran, with Khadija and Rugi behind her. She nearly bumped into Musa coming up the steps of the veranda outside.

"Look out- a snake!" she cried. He tried to take the blanket with the snake from her but she pushed him to one side. She ran down the steps and onto the drive, and threw blanket and snake as far as she could.

The snake quickly crawled out of the blanket and headed for the tall grass nearby.

Musa took a few long steps and stamped on it with one of his heavy boots. He stamped again and again and again until the snake was dead.

Then he made his way back to his mother and pulled her gently to one side.

"Musa, there's something I must tell you," she whispered . . "Khadija... "

"It's all right, Mother. I know everything and I understand. What you've done tonight has more than made up for your mistake. I know how scared you are of snakes. Does Fati know?"

His mother shook her head. "No, she doesn't. Only Khadija knows."

Musa put his arms around his mother's shoulders.

"Then this is our secret, you and me and my sisters. And the secret will be safe with us.

In the room Fati was rocking the child gently in her arms. She looked up as the four entered and smiled at them.

"Where have you all been? I was asleep and the baby cried and woke me up."

Olive went over to Fati and took the baby from her and kissed him. He stopped crying at once.

Musa and his sisters looked at each other and smiled happily.

"I feel so happy to have you all around," said Fati, still smiling.

"I was so foolish before. I don't know why I was afraid. I'm so glad you're all here, and you, too, Olive. I don't know what I would have done without you. Everything's going to be fine now, I just know it. Will you stay with me tonight?"

"I'll stay as long as you want me to," said Olive. "After all, we're all one family."

Again the three youngsters looked at each other and smiled.